D0241843

KNOWSLEY LIBRARY SERVICE

Knowsl@y Council

Please return this book on or before the date shown below

PROJECT LOAN FICTION

You may return this book to any Knowsley library
For renewal please telephone
Halewood - 486 4442   Housebound Service - 443 4223
Huyton/Mobile - 443 3734/5   Kirkby - 443 4290/89
Page Moss - 489 9814   Prescot - 426 6449
School Library Service - 443 4202
Stockbridge Village - 480 3925   Whiston - 426 4757
http://www.knowsley.gov.uk/

This
The Bear with Sticky Paws
book belongs to:

. . . .

KEEP YOUR PAWS OFF!

for Martha
with love

and for my small friend
Conrad

Knowsley Schools Library Service

3 804326974590	
Askews	06-Mar-2008
JF	£10.99
2046162	

First published in 2007
by Orchard Press
Orchard Books 338 Euston Road,
London NW1 3BH
Orchard Books Australia
Level 17/207 Kent Street, Sydney, NSW 2000
Text and illustrations © Clara Vulliamy 2007
The right of Clara Vulliamy to be identified as
the author and illustrator of this work has been
asserted by her in accordance with the
Copyright, Designs and Patents Act, 1988.
A CIP catalogue record for this book
is available from the British Library.
ISBN 978 1 84616 304 3
1 3 5 7 9 10 8 6 4 2
Printed in China
Orchard Books is a division of
Hachette Children's Books

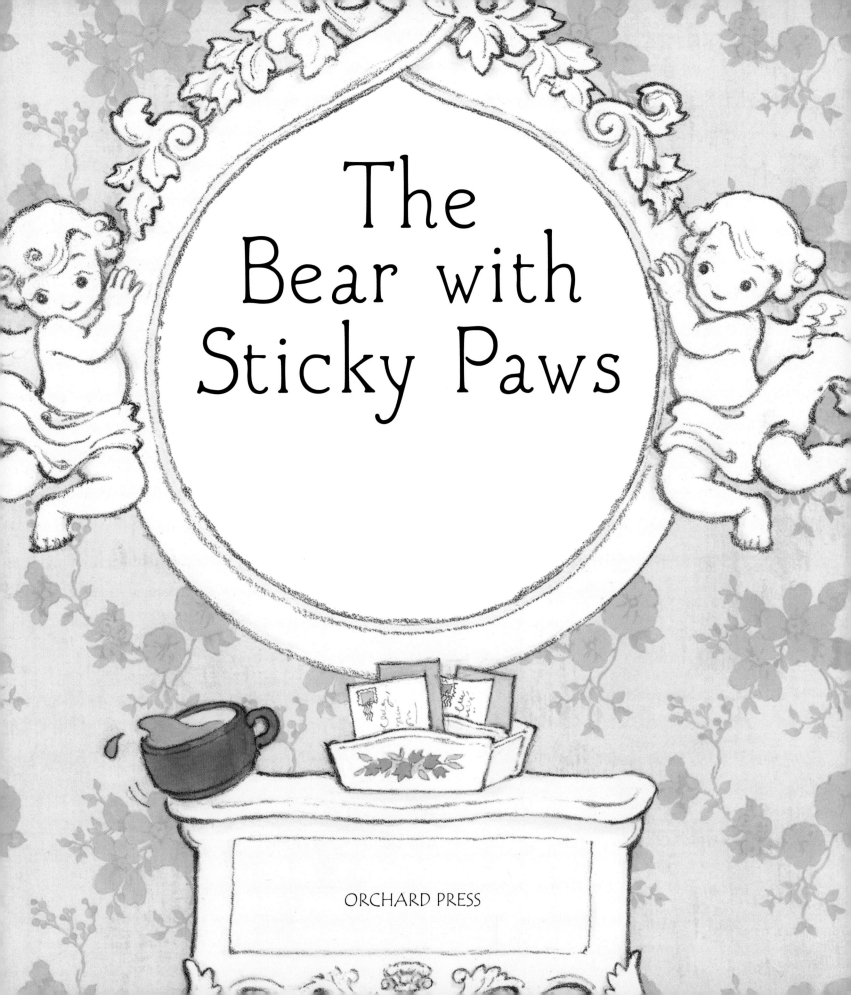

The Bear with Sticky Paws

ORCHARD PRESS

There's a girl called Pearl
and she's being very grumpy,
stamping her little feet
and slamming the door.
She says,

"I don't want all this **breakfast!**"

and throws down her spoon.

"**NO**, I won't wash my face.
NO, I won't brush my hair.
NO, I won't get dressed . . ."

"NO! NO!
NO! NO!
NO! NO!
NO! NO!
NO!"

Until Mum calls out,

"Stop!"

And –

oh NO!

She's gone!

But then,

bing-
bong!

There's a bear on the doorstep,
a small white tufty one,
standing on his suitcase to reach the bell.

"Breakfast?" says the bear,
sniffing the air.

"BREAKFAST?
Yes, please!"

The bear eats it all.
"MORE!"
says the bear.

Pearl makes

5 pancakes,

8 pieces of jammy toast

and 9 bowls of porridge.

And – oh NO!

Sticky paws everywhere!

But the bear
doesn't care . . .
"Let's PLAY!"
says the bear.

He's
snuffling
and sniffling . . .

. . . hiding
and sliding . . .

leaping
and climbing!

And –
oh NO!

He's on top of the wardrobe!

"Lunch time!" calls Pearl.
"UP HERE!" says the bear.
So Pearl has to throw the food up to him –

7 pieces of pizza,

11 carrots

and 15 sugar buns.

"Let's do dressing up!" says the bear.
"OK," says Pearl.
And – oh NO!

Down comes the curtain.

But then,
"SPARKLE!"
says the bear.
And – oh NO!
It's Mum's stuff,
too.

"Better go in the garden," says Pearl.

"SWIM!" says the bear.

And –

oh NO!

He jumps right in the fountain.

Pearl fetches tea. There are

9 honey sandwiches,

11 bowls of milk

and too many ice creams to count.

"I'm tired," says Pearl.

"NOT TIRED!" says the bear.

"Come on," says Pearl,
taking him by a sticky paw.
"It's your bedtime."

"No," says the bear.

"NO, I don't want a bath.
NO, I hate being brushed.
NO, I won't go to bed . . ."

Until Pearl calls out . . .

"STOP!"

"What about all this mess?" says Pearl.

"MESS?" says the bear.

"I don't know!

I've got to go!

GOODBYE!"

Out goes the bear.
And –

oh NO!

In comes *Mum!*

"What about all this mess?" says Mum.

And Pearl says,
"I will help tidy up.
I will wash my face.
I will brush my hair . . ."

And Pearl has
all she really wants –

1 lovely Mum,
1 huge hug
and 1 big kiss.